The Birthd

by Cynthia Swain • illustrated by Bob Taylor

Meet the Characters

Pedro

Anna

Sofia

Mom

"I will make a cake," said Anna.

"I will make a card," said Pedro.

Sofia said, "I will make some flowers!"

8

Sofia made some petals.

Sofia made red petals.

She made blue petals.

She made yellow petals.

Sofia made some stems.
Sofia made green stems.
She made leaves, too.

Pedro and Anna looked
at the flowers.
Pedro and Anna liked
the flowers.

Then Mom came home. "Happy birthday!" said the children.